SONY PICTURES
ANIMATION

ViVo™

Journey to Miami!

Adapted by Patty Michaels
Illustrated by Derek Ortega

Ready-to-Read

Simon Spotlight
New York   London   Toronto   Sydney   New Delhi

SIMON SPOTLIGHT
An imprint of Simon & Schuster Children's Publishing Division
1230 Avenue of the Americas, New York, New York 10020
This Simon Spotlight edition July 2021
TM & © 2021 Sony Pictures Animation Inc. All Rights Reserved.
All rights reserved, including the right of reproduction in whole or in
part in any form. SIMON SPOTLIGHT, READY-TO-READ, and colophon
are registered trademarks of Simon & Schuster, Inc. For information
about special discounts for bulk purchases, please contact
Simon & Schuster Special Sales at 1-866-506-1949 or
business@simonandschuster.com.
Manufactured in the United States of America 0621 LAK
10 9 8 7 6 5 4 3 2 1
ISBN 978-1-5344-7376-8 (hc)
ISBN 978-1-5344-7375-1 (pbk)
ISBN 978-1-5344-7377-5 (ebook)

This is Vivo,
an adorable kinkajou.
Vivo loved to sing
with his best friend, Andrés.

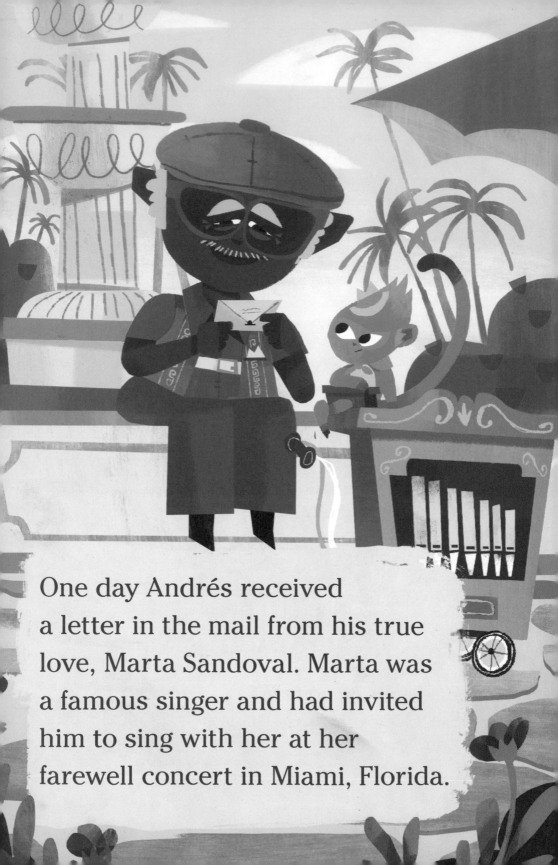

One day Andrés received a letter in the mail from his true love, Marta Sandoval. Marta was a famous singer and had invited him to sing with her at her farewell concert in Miami, Florida.

Andrés remembered all the good times
he and Marta had together.
He never had the chance to sing
the special song he wrote for her.

"Now my friend, I have
a second chance!"
he told Vivo.
"We're going to the Mambo Cabana!"

Vivo was nervous.
He did not want to leave Havana, where he and Andrés lived.
"Don't worry," Andrés said soothingly.
"Everything will be okay."

The next day Vivo
discovered something sad.
Andrés had passed away in his sleep.

"For years his music filled this plaza and our hearts," Vivo's friend Montoya said.

A few minutes later a young
girl approached Vivo.
"My name is Gabi," she said.
"You're Vivo, right?" she asked.
"My dad used to tell me a lot of
stories about you."
Andrés was Gabi's great-uncle.

"Family takes care of family,"
Gabi told Vivo.
"You should come live with me
in Florida! Come on!
Get in the bag!" she exclaimed.

Vivo did not want to go to Florida
without Andrés.
But then he read the lyrics to Andrés's
song for Marta.
Suddenly, he knew what he had to do.
He would go to Florida and deliver
the song to Marta!
Vivo jumped in Gabi's drum case to hide.

Gabi did not realize that Vivo
had snuck into her drum case
until she got home from Havana.
"Vivo, you're here!" she cried.
But Vivo was not planning on staying.
I have a song to deliver, he motioned to
Gabi.

Just then Gabi's mom knocked on
her door.
Vivo hid next to a pile of blocks.
Gabi's mom handed her a uniform.
"Hurry up and change," she told Gabi.
"We don't want to be late for the
cookie sale."

"Did you see that, Vivo?" Gabi asked him.
"She wants me to wear a uniform just like everyone else.
But I'm not *like* everyone else!"
Little did Gabi know that Vivo was not listening.
He had escaped!

Now all I have to do is find Marta, Vivo thought.

Suddenly, he spotted a bus that was going to Miami.

Mambo Cabana, here I come! he thought.

As he hopped onto the bus, he heard a loud scream.
"What is that thing?" someone shrieked.
"Shoo!" the bus driver yelled.
Just then a dog started to chase Vivo!

Luckily, Vivo was able to safely get back
to Gabi's house.

"I know why you came to Florida,"
Gabi said. "You're trying to find Marta!
I read her letter."

Vivo nodded.

"Marta's final show is tonight!" Gabi
exclaimed. "I have a plan to get you there!"

With Vivo in her backpack, Gabi biked to the bus station.

Just then she spotted a group of girls selling cookies.

"Oh no, it's the Sand Dollars!" Gabi cried.

"Gabi, where is your uniform?" one of the girls asked.

Gabi quickly came up with an excuse.
"I was busy . . . rescuing this animal,"
she said, showing them Vivo.
But the Sand Dollars didn't believe her.

"Hold on tight," Gabi told Vivo.
"Miami, here we come!" she shouted.

"I know we missed the bus," Gabi told Vivo.

"But if we take a shortcut through Everglades National Park, we can still make it!"

But a terrible storm stranded Vivo alone in a tree.

And what was even worse, the song was in Gabi's backpack!

Meanwhile, Gabi had fallen asleep on her raft.
She was awoken by . . . the Sand Dollars.
They had taken Andrés's song!
"You get the song when we have the kinkajou," one of the girls said.

Vivo was still stuck in the tree when he met a friendly bird named Dancarino.

I need your help! Vivo pleaded.
Dancarino agreed.
But then Dancarino met his own true love and flew away!

Vivo tried to chase after the birds.
He swung through a group of vines,
but one of them snapped!
He fell into a bog below.
Suddenly, something appeared in front
of him.
It was a giant python named Lutador!

Just then Dancarino came back!
"Vivo!" the bird yelled, scooping him up.
Vivo was safe!
Now he needed to find Gabi!

Meanwhile, Gabi and the Sand Dollars
were looking for Vivo.
Gabi heard a rustling noise nearby.
"Vivo?" Gabi asked hopefully.
But it wasn't Vivo.
It was . . . Lutador!

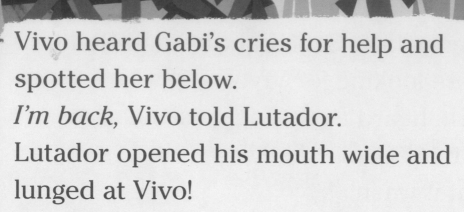

Vivo heard Gabi's cries for help and spotted her below.

I'm back, Vivo told Lutador.

Lutador opened his mouth wide and lunged at Vivo!

But the python was no match for Vivo this time.

"Vivo is a hero!" the Sand Dollars cheered.

Now Gabi and Vivo could continue
to Miami!
But there was another problem.
The paper with the song had gotten wet
and was destroyed.
I failed, Vivo thought sadly.
To Vivo's surprise Gabi started to sing
some of the lyrics.
Vivo joined in and chirped the melody.
Together they knew the full song!

Later that day Gabi finished writing down the song. "Eva, turn the boat around," Gabi told one of the Sand Dollars. "We're going to Miami!"

Soon Gabi and Vivo arrived at the Mambo Cabana!

Vivo snuck into Marta's dressing room.

Marta remembered Andrés had told her about his kinkajou.

Marta smiled. "Are you Vivo?" she asked.

Vivo nodded and handed her the song.

"Oh! I love you, too, Andrés," she said softly, reading the lyrics.

A few moments later Marta took the
stage and started to sing Andrés's
special song.

"You did it!" Gabi cheered.

Vivo shook his head and pointed at Gabi.

Gabi smiled. "You're right, *we* did it."

They had made Andrés's wish come true.